Sometimes things just come your way

Copyright © 2005 by Paula Gerritsen
Originally published by Lemniscaat b.v. Rotterdam under the title *Noten*
Printed and bound in Belgium
All rights reserved

First U.S. edition

CIP data available

Paula Gerritsen
Nuts

Front Street 8 Lemniscaat

Mouse lives on a little hill. She has
a beautiful view of the field, the farm,
the meadow, and … far, far away …
the nut tree.

Mmmm … autumn! Time to collect nuts!

Mouse wraps her scarf around her neck and puts on her coat with the big pockets. *Extra*-big pockets for *extra*-lots of nuts!

Suddenly Gull swoops above Mouse.

"Go home," he screeches. "A storm is coming."

But Mouse can't hear over the wind.

The farmer is racing back to the barn before the rain comes. Hare jumps out of the way shouting, "Get out of here, Mouse, or you'll be run over." But Mouse can't hear over the roar of the tractor.

In the meadow Sheep bleats at Mouse,
"Watch out! Behind you! A dog, a dog…!"
But Mouse can't hear over the barking.

Suddenly it gets very, very dark!
Lightning strikes and thunder roars.
The wind blows even harder.
It whips the leaves into the air and
almost lifts Mouse into the air too.

But, finally, here is the nut tree!
Mouse dives into the hole at the bottom
of the tree to get out of the wind.

And before she knows it she's fast asleep.

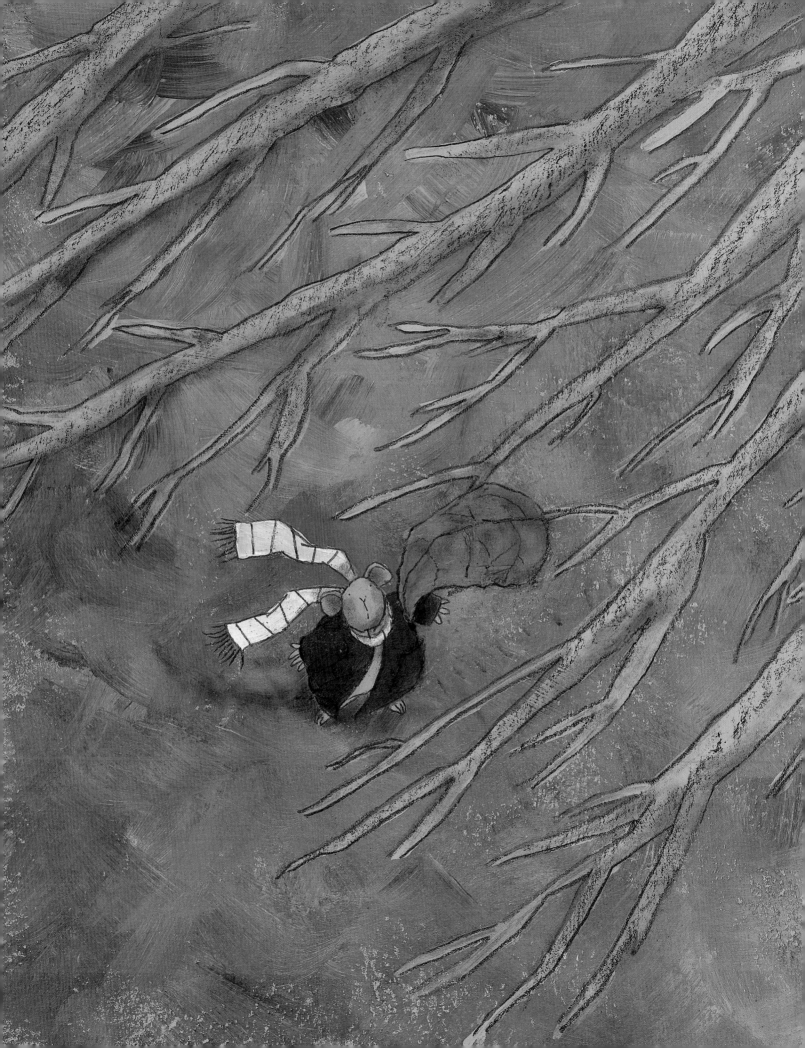

When she wakes up, Mouse goes outside to collect nuts.
But … what's happened? All the leaves are gone!
There are only two … no, three leaves left.
And all those delicious nuts are gone too.

Sadly Mouse walks home.

Back through the meadow,
back past the farm,
back through the field ...

… without one single nut in her extra-big pockets.

A few leaves fly along with her.

At home, at the top of the little hill,
Gull is jumping up and down and screeching.

"Look at the extra-special surprise
the wind brought you last night!"
says Gull with a smile.